THE STORY OF DOCTO

by HUGH LOFTING

#1 Animal Talk

Adapted by Diane Namm

Illustrated by John Kanzler

Sterling Publishing Co., Inc.
New York

Library of Congress Cataloging-in-Publication Data Available

10 9 8 7 6 5 4 3 2 1

Published by Sterling Publishing Co., Inc.
387 Park Avenue South, New York, NY 10016
Copyright © 2006 by Barnes and Noble, Inc.
Illustrations © 2006 by John Kanzler
Distributed in Canada by Sterling Publishing
c/o Canadian Manda Group, 165 Dufferin Street
Toronto, Ontario, Canada M6K 3H6
Distributed in the United Kingdom by GMC Distribution Services
Castle Place, 166 High Street, Lewes, East Sussex, England BN7 1XU
Distributed in Australia by Capricorn Link (Australia) Pty. Ltd.
P.O. Box 704, Windsor, NSW 2756, Australia

Printed in China
All rights reserved

Sterling ISBN 13: 978 1-4027-3291-1
         ISBN 10: 1-4027-3291-0

For information about custom editions, special sales, premium and
corporate purchases, please contact Sterling Special Sales
Department at 800-805-5489 or specialsales@sterlingpub.com.

Contents

Chee-Chee the Monkey

Everyone in Puddleby knew Doctor
Dolittle. He was one of the best doctors
in town. He always knew just what to
do when anyone was sick.

Doctor Dolittle loved all his patients.
They loved him, too. They brought him
good things to eat when they visited.

One day, the organ-grinder and his
monkey, Chee-Chee, came to see the
doctor. "Chee-Chee will not eat,"
the organ-grinder said.

Doctor Dolittle had never had
an animal patient, but he knew there
were no pet doctors in town.
He wanted to help.

Doctor Dolittle
checked Chee-Chee
from head to toe.

He could find
nothing wrong.

Still, Chee-Chee
would not eat.

"Let Chee-Chee stay for a while,"
Doctor Dolittle said.
"I'll see if I can help him!"

"Don't worry, little monkey,"
the doctor said. "We will find
a way to help you."

Doctor Dolittle turned to go.
As soon as he did, he heard something
he couldn't believe . . . .

A Very Special Person

"Good night," Chee-Chee said.

Doctor Dolittle was very surprised.

"Did you say 'Good night'?"
asked the doctor.

"Yes!" Chee-Chee said. "Did you
really understand me?"

"By golly, I did!" said the doctor.

"You know animal talk!"
Chee–Chee said. "You must
be a very special person."
The doctor blushed.
Then he realized something important.

"Since I can
understand you,"
said the doctor,
"you can tell me
what is wrong.
Then I can make you
feel better!"

"I ate too much yesterday."
Chee–Chee said.
"Now my tummy hurts."
"I know just the thing,"
said Doctor Dolittle.

He gave Chee-Chee
some warm soup and told
him to stay in bed.
Chee-Chee felt better
the very next day.

The monkey told some of his
friends about Doctor Dolittle.
"He knows animal talk!"
Chee-Chee said.

Chee-Chee's friends all came
to visit the wonderful doctor
who knew animal talk.

They loved the doctor
and he loved them.
One by one, he helped them all.

Animal School

Doctor Dolittle thought
this animal talk was
a strange and wonderful thing.
He wanted to know more
about it.

So after he helped
his people patients
and they went home,
he asked the animals
to stay for a while.

"Will you teach me more
about animal talk?"
the doctor asked them.
"Of course we will!"
said the animals.

Chee-Chee the monkey
taught him to chatter.

Dab-Dab the duck
taught him to quack.

Gub–Gub the pig
taught him to oink.

Jip the dog
taught him to bark.

Polynesia the parrot
taught him
to squawk.

The animals also told

the doctor secrets animals know.

They taught him
special animal cures
and other things
only animals know.

A Wonderful Idea

It took a long time
for Doctor Dolittle to learn
all the things the animals
had to teach.
Meanwhile, the people
of Puddleby went to other doctors
when they needed help.

When Doctor Dolittle
opened his office again,
his people patients didn't need him
anymore. "I miss them!" he said.
"So do we!" said the animals.

"Let's sit down and eat,
and talk about how
to get them back,"
the doctor said.
He opened the cupboard,

but his people patients
had not been to visit
with good things to eat—
and it was bare!

Luckily, Chee-Chee had an idea.
"The town needs a pet doctor,"
he told Doctor Dolittle. "*You* can be
our pet doctor. People will bring
food when they bring their pets!"

Doctor Dolittle thought
this was a wonderful idea.
So he hung a sign outside.
The sign said Pet Doctor.

Soon the people of Puddleby
were bringing in their pets
and good things to eat.
The doctor was so happy
to be helping Puddleby again.
The town was happy, too,
for Doctor Dolittle
always knew just what to do.